Cupcakes fit for a superhero?

Horace stared at the cupcakes on the plate. "Yowee-zowee-zooks!" he exclaimed. "Are you sure you made those right?" Each cupcake was different from the next, but none of them looked like it should be eaten. One was gray with crumbly, spotted pebble things on top. The second was completely black. It looked as if it were made from coal. The third was white and had all these little shiny needles poking out through the icing. The last one was a swirling mix of black and brown cake with what at first looked like chocolate icing, but then when Horace leaned in close, he could see that it was really thousands of tiny wriggling black worms.

"Which one will you try first?" Melody asked.

For Christopher Robison or
Augusten X. Burroughs

—*L.D.*

THE CUPCAKED CRUSADER

by Lawrence David

illustrated by Barry Gott

PUFFIN BOOKS

To Rose and Finn

—*B.G.*

PUFFIN BOOKS
Published by the Penguin Group
Penguin Putnam Books for Young Readers,
345 Hudson Street, New York, New York 10014, U.S.A.
Penguin Books Ltd, 80 Strand, London WC2R ORL, England
Penguin Books Australia Ltd, Ringwood, Victoria, Australia
Penguin Books Canada Ltd, 10 Alcorn Avenue, Toronto, Ontario, Canada M4V 3B2
Penguin Books (N.Z.) Ltd, 182-190 Wairau Road, Auckland 10, New Zealand

Penguin Books Ltd, Registered Offices: Harmondsworth, Middlesex, England

Published simultaneously by Dutton Children's Books
and Puffin Books, divisions of Penguin Putnam Books for Young Readers, 2002

5 7 9 10 8 6

LIBRARY OF CONGRESS CATALOGING-IN-PUBLICATION DATA
David, Lawrence. Horace Splattly: the cupcaked crusader / by Lawrence David;
illustrated by Barry Gott.—1st ed.   p.   cm.   "Book one"
Summary: When his little sister's magic cupcakes transform him into a flying,
fire-breathing superhero, ten-year-old Horace Splattly has adventures that
include confronting the monster at the school playground.
[1. Heroes—Fiction. 2. Brothers and sisters—Fiction. 3. Monsters—Fiction.
4. Schools—Fiction. 5. Humorous stories.] I. Gott, Barry, ill. II. Title.
PZ7.L43534 Ho 2002 [Fic]—dc21 2001023966

ISBN 0-525-46763-7 (hardcover)

ISBN 0-14-230021-7 (pbk.)

Printed in the United States of America

Contents

Chapter 1

THE ALMOST SHORTEST KID IN BLOOTINVILLE ELEMENTARY

Horace Splattly stared long and hard across the school yard. "How can we find out if it's true?" he asked his two best friends. He looked at the dirt under his feet. "Do you think maybe we can find a footprint?"

The sun shined brightly on this early spring Tuesday in Blootinville. All the kids at Blootinville Elementary were outside on the playground. Some played on the swings. Others jumped rope, played hopscotch, or chased each other until they got sick and fell in the dirt, holding their stomachs, full of lunch.

Still, ten-year-old Horace Splattly could not take his eyes off the ground. He kept walking across the yard, zigzagging between the kids. He spied lots of small, kid footprints. He saw a few larger, adult footprints, but no giant, animal footprints.

Auggie (sounds like "oggy") and Xax (sounds like "zacks"), Horace's twin best friends, trailed after him. The only way anyone could tell the Blootin twins apart was that Auggie had a birthmark in the shape of a crab on his right wrist, and Xax had one on his left wrist. The town was named after their family.

"Maybe the monster doesn't live around here," Auggie Blootin said, brushing his blond bangs back over his head.

"Maybe it doesn't have any feet to make footprints," Xax Blootin said, shaking his blond bangs over his eyes and peering down through them at Horace.

At a height of only thirty inches, Horace was no taller than a large sack of Puppy Chow dog food. In fact, Horace was the shortest kid in Blootinville Elementary except for the kinder-

gartners and six of the first graders. Of course, that didn't stop him from having some of the biggest and wildest ideas possible. Horace brushed his palm across the top of his short, spiky hair. It stuck up in the air like a field of black weeds. Horace's parents let him cut it himself. "I told you I saw it last night when my mom was driving me home from your house. There was a man standing right here playing with a giant, hairy monster. It was as large as a school bus. The man was trying to teach the monster to play fetch."

Auggie and Xax stood side by side, their lanky bodies like two fence posts. Their heads bobbed in unison as they thought about their friend's story.

"Maybe it was just a shadow," Auggie said.

"If there was no sun, how could it be a shadow?" Horace asked.

"Maybe you just imagined it up," Xax said, hoping his friend was wrong.

Horace leaned against the red brick that

made up their prison, otherwise known as elementary school. "Come on, guys, we have a lot more of this playground to cover before recess is over. There has to be evidence of the monster out here somewhere."

The three boys turned their gazes to the ground.

"Anything exciting going on in the dirt today?" someone joked.

Xax, Auggie, and Horace looked up from the ground to see their principal standing over them and smiling brightly. Principal Nosair was a big man with curly brown hair that drooped in his eyes. He always wore a bright orange coat and yellow-and-orange-striped pants. The boys thought he looked more like a circus clown than a principal.

"Uh, no, sir," Xax said. "We're not looking for anything. We're just being as good as we possibly can be."

Principal Nosair nodded. He peered down at the dirt. "Lose something?"

"No," Horace said. "We were just looking for large animal footprints."

Auggie and Xax shot Horace angry looks and shook their shaggy blond heads at him. A frown came across Principal Nosair's face. He knelt on the ground. His green eyes were level with the boys' eyes. He leaned in close to them and slowly shook his head back and forth. "Oh, children, children," he said. "You shouldn't be snooping around after large monstrous creatures. Heaven knows what might happen if you found one. A monster could eat you in one single bite." The principal chomped his mouth open and closed.

Xax swallowed a lump in his throat.

Auggie's jaw dropped.

Horace's eyes opened as big as saucers. "Do you mean there really is a monster that comes out on the playground?" Horace asked. "I thought I saw—"

Principal Nosair stood. "One monster, two monsters, maybe three monsters—one for each

of you." He smiled and reached down to ruf-
fle Horace's hair. "Please, boys. Monsters at
school? Do you really think that's possible? Just
ask my brother. He can tell you that no giant
monsters exist in Blootinville. Especially not
in our school yard." The principal walked off
across the playground to stop a group of four
girls from tying all their pigtails together.

"I can't believe you told him, Horace," Auggie
said. "It was supposed to be a secret."

"I didn't tell him what I saw. I only asked a

question," Horace replied. He gazed at the ground and put the forefinger of his left hand on his chin, then the forefinger of his right hand in his ear and twisted it in a circle.

Xax and Auggie knew this look. The last time Horace had it, he had decided that their goody-two-shoes classmate Myrna Breckstein was really an adult because she carried a lady's large straw handbag just like Horace's mom did. Horace was absolutely, totally, positively positive that their teachers had hired Myrna to pose as a ten-year-old kid to spy on them. To prove he was right, he convinced Xax and Auggie to help him kidnap the adult-girl.

They took Myrna into the janitor's closet and interrogated her while a wet mop dripped on her head. All that happened was that Myrna wet her pants, and Auggie, Xax, and Horace had to clean the boys' bathroom during recess for two whole weeks. Finally, Horace admitted that Myrna wasn't really a grown-up, just a big baby with a large straw purse.

So this time, watching Horace contemplating the playground monster, Xax and Auggie immediately became worried.

"Come on, Horace," Xax pleaded. "I don't want to clean any more bathrooms. What are you thinking?"

"I *am* thinking," Horace said. "And what I'm thinking is maybe Principal Nosair is right. Maybe Mr. Dienow can help us find out if there really are monsters in Blootinville. After all, he is the science teacher."

Principal Nosair was Mr. Dienow's older half brother. They had the same mother but different fathers. After Tyler Nosair became principal of Blootinville Elementary, he hired his brother, Norman Dienow, to be the science teacher. All the kids liked Principal Nosair, but not one kid liked Mr. Dienow. He smelled like old cheese that had sat on the kitchen counter all summer, and he talked to the kids with a voice as loud and angry as a Weedwacker. But not one kid had ever complained to their parents or Principal

Nosair about Mr. Dienow, because they were afraid of him and he was the principal's brother.

"You can't ask Dienow anything ever," Auggie said. "Remember what happened when Francine Hoboken asked if the earth went around the sun or the sun around the earth?"

"Yeah," Xax said. "He painted Francine's face yellow and his own blue and green."

"And then he tied her to a pole and started dancing around her, singing, 'I'm the earth and you're the sun! I'm the earth and you're the sun!'" Auggie said.

Xax dropped his head into his hands and shook it back and forth. "Just imagine what he'll do if you ask him about monsters on the playground," he warned.

Horace gasped. "Yowee-zowee-zooks!" He knelt on the ground and waved a hand. "Look at this, you guys."

Chapter 2

DOUGHNUTS, FISH, AND THE WALRUS

Xax and Auggie squatted beside Horace. There, in a patch of dried mud, was a giant footprint of some kind of animal. It had a large heel, four toes, and four long, sharp claws that dug deep into the soil. Horace lay on his back inside the footprint. It fit him well and felt kind of comfortable. It was as wide as Horace was tall and as long as Horace was wide when he stretched his arms as far as he could.

Horace sat up in the paw print. "Something evil could be going on out here every night," Horace declared. "A monster could be hiding and waiting to attack everyone."

"It does seem sort of monsterlike," Auggie agreed. "But you can't really know for sure."

Xax shook with fear. "Do you think maybe some kids did it as a prank?"

"When we get back to the classroom, we need to immediately enter this information into *The Splattly and Blootin Big Notebook of Worldwide Conspiracies*," Horace ordered. "This could be a plan by some group of people to do something really evil."

Whenever Horace, Xax, and Auggie spied anything suspicious (and they were *always* spying suspicious things), they entered their thoughts into *The Splattly and Blootin Big Notebook of Worldwide Conspiracies*. Sometimes they would investigate by snooping around. Sometimes they wore disguises. And sometimes they went on the Internet and asked people if they had any answers to their mysteries. Last week, the three friends were positive that Mr. Howlly at the doughnut shop was really a talking walrus (after all, he looked just like one) .

To prove they were right, the boys dressed up like fish, wearing gray sweatshirts, sweatpants, and ski hats. The plan was that they would run into the doughnut shop, lie down on the floor, and flap their bodies up and down like fish out of water. When Mr. Howlly tried to eat them, they would take a picture and prove he was a walrus.

What happened was the boys ran into the shop, lay down on the floor, and flapped around, just as they'd planned. Customers ran from the store, scared of the wild children. Mr. Howlly screamed at the boys. His bushy mustache twitched, and he bared his big teeth. Auggie, Xax, and Horace were sure he would soon be on his hands and knees, slithering across the floor toward them like a walrus on ice. But before that happened, just as the boys *hadn't* planned, Mayor A. X. Blootin, the twins' father, walked into the doughnut shop and found Mr. Howlly yelling at his sons and Horace. He quickly pulled the boys to their feet and forbade them from ever setting foot in the doughnut shop again.

The boys realized they might never know if Mr. Howlly was a doughnut-making walrus or not.

Now they had found a large monster footprint stamped onto the playground.

Horace circled the print. "We'll make our notes, then we can begin our investigation and ask Mr. Dienow what he thinks."

Auggie held up his hands. "I don't think so, Horace. After what happened in the doughnut shop and when we kidnapped Myrna, our dad doesn't want us to go on any investigations without checking with him first. Remember, Xax?"

"Remember what?" Xax asked. The night after the boys had been caught at the doughnut shop, the Blootin twins' dad told them not to do what Horace said without telling him first. But Xax had been too busy counting the chocolate chips in his dessert to pay attention to what his father said. Xax always had to count the chocolate chips in his cookies before he could eat them. That usually meant everyone else had already finished their cookies and licked the crumbs from their plates before he'd even taken one bite.

"We have to do something," Horace said, standing up. "We can't just let the monster take over the school. Maybe if we ask Mr. Dienow—"

"No way!" Auggie exclaimed. "Horace, you're our friend and the triplet Xax and I never had, but you can't tell anyone. Look at that footprint," he said. "It's just a big blot in the dirt. You don't know that it's from a monster. The number-one rule of *The Splattly and Blootin Big Notebook of Worldwide Conspiracies* is that we don't share anything with anyone until we have proof."

Horace looked at Auggie, and Auggie looked at Xax. Xax looked at his watch. "One, two, three, four, five, six, and—" Xax counted quietly, then held up a hand, pointing a finger at the bell by the school door.

Brrrrrring—brrrrrrrring!

Recess was over. Auggie, Xax, and Horace began walking toward the door, where Principal Nosair stood, smiling.

Horace took one more long and hard look at the footprint. "I think we do have enough proof," he muttered under his breath. "I think this monster is going to be very, very dangerous."

Chapter 3

QUESTIONS AND NO ANSWERS

Horace had to get through history, math, and PE before he had science class with Mr. Dienow. And the longer he waited to ask the science teacher about the playground monster, the more certain he became that the monster was planning to attack the kids at school. In fact, the only thing that took Horace's mind off thinking about the monster was a girl holding a large, red rubber ball.

In PE, they played dodgeball. Half the class stood against a wall, and the other half pitched large, red rubber balls at them. Sara Willow stood opposite the wall, wearing her pink-and-white-striped shirt with a pink bow on each shoulder and matching pink skirt with a big bow on the belt. Her henna-rinsed pigtails spilled over her shoulders. Every day she wore her hair in a new style, and often with a new hair color. Sara held a red rubber ball to her chest, preparing to throw it at one of her classmates.

Horace stood next to Xax and Auggie. He couldn't take his eyes off Sara. She looked as pretty to him as fresh dirt looked to an earthworm.

"Horace, watch out!" Auggie called.

Sara's ball shot forward and hit Horace square in the middle of his shirt.

"Horace is out! Horace is out!" Sara shrieked, jumping for joy, pigtails whipping around her like the arms of a carnival ride.

Horace proudly strode away from the wall and over to Mr. Fisk, the gym teacher. "This was my hundredth time to be the first kid hit," he told his teacher, smiling.

Mr. Fisk gave Horace a pat on the shoulder.

"I don't know what you're made of, Horace, but you sure do seem like a red-rubber-ball magnet."

• • •

Mr. Dienow stood before the class in his long white lab coat, ruby-red pants, and cowboy boots. His stringy white hair was pulled tight behind his head in a ponytail. He held his thin head up, his pointy chin high in the air. His deep gray eyes gazed hatefully at the small tomato

plant in his hands. It had three leaves and one little red tomato. "This horrible vine is an example of a tomato plant," Mr. Dienow explained in a scratchy voice. "It is little and scrawny and ugly and grows tomatoes the size of peas." He took a second tomato plant from behind his desk and set it beside the normal plant. The second plant's thick green vines nearly reached the ceiling. It had hundreds of leaves and dozens of ruby-red tomatoes the size of baseballs.

"What happened to that tomato plant?" Sara Willow asked. "It looks much prettier."

"Not *prettier*, Sara," Mr. Dienow replied in a nasty tone. "*Lusher*. More full of life. This plant has been given special chemicals I created to make it bigger. The moral of this, children, is that bigger is better and that I am smarter than you. Make sure you remember that I am smarter than you. It will be on next week's test."

Horace sighed. Who cared about tomato plants? He didn't even like small tomatoes. Why would he want bigger ones? There were much more important things in life than tomatoes. *Monsters* were much more important. Horace raised an arm in the air.

Mr. Dienow looked out across the classroom. "Any questions?"

Horace stretched his hand higher. He was the only one with a hand in the air.

"Since no one has any questions, I want you to read Chapter Eight of your science book, all about tomato plants," Mr. Dienow said. "When you finish with Chapter Eight, read Chapter

Nine, which is also about tomato plants."

The kids began opening their textbooks.

"Mr. Dienow," Horace called. "I have a question."

Mr. Dienow gazed across the fourth-grade students. "Who's talking? Where's that voice coming from?"

Cyrus Splinter laughed and pointed at Horace. Cyrus was the tallest boy in all of Blootinville Elementary by half a foot, and the meanest by ten and a half yards. "Little-bitty-baby Horace Splattly has his hand up. He's just so tiny you can't see him."

"I may have a little body, but my brain's twice as big as yours," Horace said.

The class laughed. Cyrus glared at Horace.

Mr. Dienow raised his chin in the air and pointed at Horace. "Stand on your desk so everyone can see you."

Horace stood atop his desk and held his arms out to the sides to keep his balance.

The science teacher grinned. "What's your name? Have you always been in this class?"

"Yes, sir. I'm Horace Splattly. I'm just short for my age."

Mr. Dienow nodded. "Yes, I can see that. Well, well. You're about as small as that puny tomato plant." He smiled and looked at the other students. "Maybe I should give Horace some of my special chemicals so he can grow."

All the kids laughed, even Sara Willow. The only ones who didn't were Auggie and Xax. Horace's face turned bright red. His cheeks burned. "Horace, sit down," Auggie whispered.

"What do you have to say, Horace? Any *little* question you have to ask?" Mr. Dienow said.

Horace tried to keep himself from shaking. He could feel the eyes of his classmates upon him. He was sure if he acted smart, then Sara Willow would really like him, and not just throw red rubber balls at his stomach.

Mr. Dienow threw a piece of chalk across the room, striking a poster of the human body in the neck. "Speak up! Everyone's waiting to hear your important question, little boy."

Horace opened his mouth and let the words spill out. "Mr. Dienow, at recess Principal Nosair said Auggie, Xax, and I could ask you if you think there could be a giant monster-beast in the school yard. I thought I saw one last night."

"You're the only monster-beast I've ever seen, shrimpy," Cyrus Splinter teased.

All the kids laughed and hooted. Auggie and Xax moaned and hid their faces in their hands. Kids poked the twins with their pencils and tossed crumpled balls of paper at their heads.

"Quiet down! All of you!" Mr. Dienow shouted.

The class fell completely silent. The only sound Horace heard was from Chipper, the class guinea pig. He rested in his small glass cage, chewing on the bulb of a celernip. Mr. Dienow leaned across his desk, his deep gray eyes growing red with rage. "Mr. Splattly, I'd advise you to keep your questions about playground monsters to yourself and your nose in your textbook. *Don't waste my time*. My brother should have known better than to encourage you to ask me such a foolish, stupid question. Now sit down."

Horace didn't sit down. He remained standing on his desk. "You don't have to be so mean about it," he said in a quiet voice.

"What was that?" Mr. Dienow asked.

Horace spoke louder. "You don't have to be so mean. I was just asking a question. Aren't we supposed to ask questions in school? I may not be able to make my body bigger than most kids', but I can try to learn more and make my brain smarter than anyone else's."

All the kids in the classroom gasped.

Mr. Dienow clenched his hands into tight fists. "Sit down, you stupid boy," he hissed.

Horace shook with fear, but he remained standing on his desk. "I am not a stupid boy," he said. "You're a mean man, and I'm going to tell your brother that you're a bad teacher."

Mr. Dienow pounded a fist on his desk. "Sit down!" he roared.

Three loud rings filled the air. The end of the school day had arrived.

Uncurling his fingers, Mr. Dienow pointed to the door. "Class is dismissed! Go home, you rotten tomatoes! Get out of here!"

The kids gathered their things and dashed from the classroom as fast as they could, backpacks swinging, skateboards rolling, sneakers trotting, and cell phones ringing.

Horace climbed down from his desk. On his way out of the room, he stopped for a quick look at Chipper. He was a small guinea pig with long black, brown, and white hair that flowed over his body and onto the floor of his cage.

Chipper stared at Horace with shiny black eyes.

"I hope Mr. Dienow treats you better than he treats us," Horace said.

Chipper opened his mouth and growled.

"Stay away from my pet," Mr. Dienow warned. The teacher shoved Horace toward the door, then reached into the cage and scratched the guinea pig's back. As Horace walked toward the exit, he passed the special tomato plant and stopped. At the beginning of the class, it had almost reached the ceiling, and the tomatoes had been the size of baseballs. Now the plant was only a couple of feet taller than Horace, and the tomatoes were the size of golf balls. Horace shook his head and wondered if he needed glasses.

WHAT SWEET MELODY IS THIS?

Auggie and Xax stood on the sidewalk outside the school as kids ran to their buses, bicycles, scooters, and rides.

Horace raced over to his friends, waving his arms frantically. "How'd I do?" he asked. "How did Sara react?"

Auggie and Xax scowled.

"What's up?" Horace asked. "You're looking at me as if I dropped tarantulas in your underpants."

Cyrus Splinter walked by with a group of his friends. He reached down and poked the top of Horace's, Xax's, and Auggie's heads. "These guys think a monster lives on the playground!" he said, and laughed.

"Does the monster like to go on the swings?" Michael Ma joked.

"Hey," Horace called. He reached into his backpack and pulled out *The Splattly and Blootin Big Notebook of Worldwide Conspiracies*. "We have a whole book of weird stuff and—"

Auggie swiped the book from Horace. Xax clamped a hand over Horace's mouth.

"Losers," Cyrus jeered. The boys walked off, laughing.

Horace pulled away from Xax and grabbed the book from Auggie. "What's wrong with you guys? You didn't even help me out. You believe in this stuff as much as I do. Xax, remember how you think there's a dragon in a cave under your house?"

"But there is," Xax argued. "Mom said the builders saw Gretel when they built the house a hundred years ago. She breathes fire and—"

"Will you be quiet!" Auggie snapped, then glared at Horace. "So what if we believe some of this stuff? That doesn't mean you should tell everyone. First in front of the class and now showing them our book? You know these are all secret."

Horace stomped his foot on the pavement, raising a puff of dust. "I was just letting everyone know so they'd be prepared in case—"

"Ha!" Auggie exclaimed. "You were just showing off in front of Sara. And it didn't work, because now she thinks you're dorky."

"The whole class thinks we're dorky," Xax said.

"But it's for a good reason," Horace argued.

Auggie looked from Horace to Xax. "Home, twin?"

Xax looked from Horace to Auggie. "Twin, home?"

Horace looked at the identical-twin Blootin brothers. They scowled at him, their hair falling over their eyes. "I thought we were supposed to be trips, right? Aren't I the triplet you never had?" Horace asked.

"Horace! Horace! Horace!" The familiar cry came from behind him.

Horace turned to see Melody, his second-grade sister. She clutched her lavender Lily Deaver tote bag to her side and was wearing the matching Lily Deaver shoes, scarf, hairband, gloves, and opera glasses. Her dark brown hair hung straight down to her shoulders, then flipped up in a large, tight curl. Melody held the opera glasses up to her eyes and peered at her brother closely. "I see a cobweb of wrinkles forming around your eyes. Perhaps you need a batch of my cucumber-radish paste for a soothing facial mask?"

"I don't need any beauty creams!" Horace snapped. "I'm talking to my friends and—"

Melody peered over Horace's shoulder. As she was seven inches taller than her older brother, it was very easy. "Friends? I don't see *any* friends behind you, little brother." She let the opera glasses hang from a chain around her neck.

Horace turned to witness Auggie and Xax walking away down the street. "Darn it," he exclaimed. "I can't believe they left without saying good-bye."

Melody tilted her head to the side. "Oh, Horace, please, let's go home. I have to work on my cupcake experiment and spy on Penny Honey to see what she's going to create for our history diorama project. *And* I have to prepare dinner for the family. It's not easy baking four full dinners in my Lily Deaver Cook & Bake Oven, you know." Melody marched off.

Horace followed slowly, turning his head from side to side as he walked up the hill to the Splattly home, taking in the view of the town. Blootinville was named after Auggie and Xax's great-, great-, not-so-great, pretty-good grand-mother, Serena Blootin. She had founded the town one hundred and eighty-three years, four months, and two days ago. Blootins had been the mayors of Blootinville ever since.

In school, all the kids had to memorize the major events of the town's history. Such as how on January 20, 1963, the town of Blootinville disappeared for an entire day. No one knew how or why it had happened. Horace, Xax, and Auggie were waiting for it to happen again so they could solve the mystery.

Because when it did, they were going to take

pictures of it. If disappearing towns show up on film.

And if the twins would ever speak to him again.

Horace wished they didn't feel they had to keep their notebook a secret. He knew that once they solved one of the mysteries, they'd become the town heroes. Why couldn't Xax and Auggie understand that? Why couldn't they be as proud of all their investigations as he was? Weren't they happy they lived in a town that had so many mysteries to solve?

Horace glanced off to the east of town to the large celernip farm that Cyrus Splinter's father had planted. The first settlers in Blootinville had been celery and turnip farmers. Then one day, Leroy Splinter crossed a celery stalk with a turnip and created the celernip. The new vegetable put Blootinville on the map, and to celebrate, every summer the annual Blootinville Celernip Festival was held. All the ten- to fourteen-year-old boys vied to become Celernip Prince. This would be Horace's first year entering the contest. Melody wanted to train him to sing and juggle while hopping on a pogo stick and wearing a grass hula skirt.

Horace thought not.

He turned his head to the south, where the Blootinville International Airport & Town Dump stood. People from all around the world came to town to throw away their trash. Last week, he, Xax, and Auggie had gone down there and found four Japanese paper lanterns, a pair of wooden shoes from the Netherlands, and a ten-foot-tall replica of the Eiffel Tower made entirely out of chewed-bubble-gum wads.

Horace and his sister reached their street at the top of the hill. It was supposed to be named Hill Top Road, but the painter had bungled the job and no one wanted to pay to have a new sign made.

Horace glanced up at the sign marking the street.

Hip Hop Toad.

Chapter 5

HIP HOP TOAD

At the corner of Hip Hop Toad, Melody lifted her opera glasses to her eyes. She peered across the street to Penny Honey's three-story yellow house with the white picket fence and half-circle driveway. She moaned, just as she did every day when they passed her house.

In the middle of Penny Honey's front lawn stood a gold mermaid fountain. The mermaid posed on a rock and held a fish that spit a stream of water high in the air. Where the sunlight caught the spray, a rainbow appeared.

Melody gasped. "I don't know why we have to have a straight, ordinary driveway and a plain old grass lawn with no fountain," she whined.

The roar of a helicopter filled the air. Horace

and Melody looked up to see a green-and-yellow-striped flying machine swoop over their heads and land on the roof of the Honeys' home. Penny leaped onto the heliport. The helicopter took off into the air and flew away. Penny waved to the Splattlys. "Hiya-doodle, Melody," she yelled from the rooftop.

Melody forced a smile. "Hiya-doodle, Penny."

Penny giggled and slung her mink-fur backpack over her shoulder. "I'm just about to start work on my historical diorama," she called. "Mine's going to have lights, an explosion, and make use of the latest in top-secret robotic technology. What's yours going to be?"

Melody swallowed and got a lump in her throat. "Mine's—mine's a secret," she shouted back to Penny.

"Can't wait to see it," Penny called cheerfully, and she stepped into the elevator that took her down into her house.

The minute Penny was out of sight, Melody frowned. "That Penny Honey thinks she's so special. I have more Lily Deaver troop badges than she does."

Horace shrugged. "I think she seems perfectly nice."

Melody poked Horace again. "What do you know? You may be two years older than me, but I'm two times as smart." She ran down the street ahead of her brother. Horace didn't bother to chase after her. He just strolled up the street, smiling when the Splattlys' house came into view.

The Splattlys might not live on the richest block with the biggest homes, but Horace thought theirs *was* the nicest house in the nicest neighborhood in all of Blootinville. It was a white house with bright red shutters and a bright red door with a large brass door knocker in the shape of a bull's head with a ring through its nose.

Today, instead of the bull, Horace saw his sister standing in the doorway, wearing her lavender Lily Deaver lab coat and gloves. She clutched a lavender Lily Deaver spatula in her hand. A dollop of cupcake batter sat on its tip. "Come inside, Horace," she ordered. "You can change out of your school clothes, then I'd like to see you in the kitchen."

Horace stared at his younger sister. "You're not Mom, and you only just turned eight, so back off." He walked past Melody and into the house, a frown on his face. "I told you I'm not going to let you test your experiments on me. No way." He tossed his backpack onto the living-room carpet.

Melody followed after him. "Oh, you're not?" She pointed the spatula at Horace's nose.

Horace looked at the batter on its tip. Hmmm . . . "What kind of cupcakes are you making?" he asked.

Melody smiled. "Fantastically delicious ones, of course."

Horace's stomach rumbled with hunger. "Well, if they look good, *maybe* I'll let you give me just one," he said.

"I thought you might," Melody said, and she clapped the spatula to her palm, sending a smattering of batter across Horace's face.

SPAGHETTI-AND-MEATBALL BATHS

Horace wiped his face on his sleeve, picked up his backpack, and trudged upstairs. Why did everyone think they could pick on him just because he was short? Mr. Dienow, Cyrus Splinter, Melody . . . And when he tried to show everyone how smart he was, Auggie and Xax got mad at him. First thing tomorrow before school, he'd march right into Principal Nosair's office and tell him how mean Dienow had been to him in class.

But Mr. Dienow was Principal Nosair's younger brother. Would Principal Nosair believe Horace if he told on Dienow? No one had ever done that before. Everyone had always been afraid to.

Horace tossed his backpack on his bedroom floor and stomped one foot. . . . If he could only *prove* the monster existed, then everyone would believe him, even Sara Willow. And Xax and Auggie wouldn't be upset anymore. But how would he ever be able to do that?

Horace changed into a T-shirt and a pair of gym pants with stripes down the sides. He put his high-tops back on and glanced at his clock radio with the built-in tissue holder, toothpaste dispenser, and bird feeder. Sometimes Horace would set the contraption on the windowsill and watch as bluebirds and sparrows sat on the clock, listened to music, and ate the seed. Once a robin accidentally hit the toothpaste dispenser and ended up with some tartar-control white-brightening spearmint gel all over its beak.

Horace checked the clock. Three-thirty on a Tuesday meant that Dad would be meeting with Chef Quaquaqua, the school-cafeteria cook.

Horace snuck downstairs into the living room and sat on the floor by the back-wall air vent. Dad's office was the next room over and had a separate entrance and driveway for the patients.

When Horace pressed his ear against the steel grille, he could hear some of what Chef Quaquaqua was telling his dad.

"For the past three weeks ... I've taken baths in a large tub filled with spaghetti and meatballs," the chef said. ". . . skin is turning orange . . ."

"How do you feel about that?" Horace's dad asked.

Horace's dad was Dr. Hinkle Splattly, a psychiatrist. People met with him for many different reasons. Sometimes they just wanted to discuss their feelings about not being happy with their jobs or friends or families. Other times it was to solve a problem, like Chef Quaquaqua, who couldn't stop taking spaghetti-and-meatball baths.

Horace wished he could have told Xax and Auggie of the chef's troubles, but he knew that his dad's meetings with his patients were top

secret, even more top secret than *The Splattly and Blootin Big Notebook of Worldwide Conspiracies.*

Chef Quaquaqua said more. ". . . after school last night . . . sunset . . . saw a giant mon—"

"Horace! Come in here!" Melody called from the kitchen.

Horace pressed his ear hard against the grille. Was the chef saying he saw a monster at sunset on the playground just like he himself had?

"Horace!"

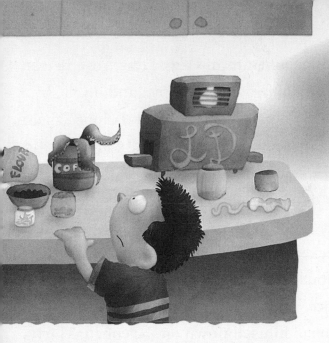

"All right," he told his sister. He stood, trying to decide what he should do. Maybe tomorrow during lunch he could ask the chef if he'd seen anything unusual on the playground recently. Then Xax and Auggie would definitely believe him.

Horace went into the kitchen. Melody stood at the table with four different bowls of batter and an assortment of flour, sugar, food coloring, and icings. Lined up along the counter were baby-food jars filled with dead flies, rubber bands, mashed Gummi Bears, dirt, rose petals, dimes, shoelaces, pencil tips, and eyelashes. Melody held a pair of tweezers and dipped them into one of the jars, then added something to one of the bowls of batter.

"There we go," she said to herself. She looked up. "I'm going to have a cupcake for you in"— she checked her Lily Deaver cooking timer— "thirty-four seconds."

Horace sighed, went into the family room, and plopped himself down on the couch. Thirty-four seconds later, Melody entered the room with a plateful of the four weirdest-looking cupcakes Horace had ever seen.

Chapter 7

YOWEE-ZOWEE-ZOOKS!

Horace stared at the cupcakes on the plate. "Yowee-zowee-zooks!" he exclaimed. "Are you sure you made those right?" Each cupcake was different from the next, but none of them looked like it should be eaten. One was gray with crumbly, spotted pebble things on top. The second was completely black. It looked as if it were made from coal. The third was white and had all these little shiny needles poking out through the icing. The last one was a swirling mix of black and brown cake with what at first looked like chocolate icing, but then when Horace leaned in close, he could see that it was really thousands of tiny wriggling black worms.

"Which one will you try first?" Melody asked.

"I've been working on them since I got my oven last year. I think I've finally got them perfect."

Horace's mouth dropped open. "You think these are *perfect*? They look like you found them on the side of the road."

Melody set the plate down on the coffee table and tilted her head. "Hmmm, I suppose you're right. There is something missing."

Horace nodded, relieved. "I'm glad you've come to your senses."

Melody nodded. "No, you're right. You certainly can't eat the cupcakes yet. At least, not without a refreshing glass of Splinter Farm celernip juice." She strode off to the kitchen to get her brother a drink.

Horace stared at the cupcakes. If he worked fast, maybe he could run to the bathroom and flush them down the toilet.

"Hey, kids, what's going on?" Dr. Splattly opened the front door and clapped his hands. "How's everyone doing?" Horace and Melody's father checked on the kids between sessions with his patients. Mari Splattly, their mother, worked as the publisher of the *Blootinville Banner*, and she usually didn't get home until 7:00 P.M.

Horace stood, holding the plate. "Hi, Dad," he said. "I was just—"

Dr. Splattly looked down at the cupcakes. "You taking care of your sister and helping her out with her cooking project? What a good older brother."

Melody walked into the hall with a glass of celernip juice. "Hi, Daddy," she said. She kissed his cheek. "Horace and I are playing."

Dr. Splattly reached for the brown-and-black cupcake. "Can I play, too?"

Horace backed away. He didn't want his father to get sick and die from Melody's experiment. It was bad enough that he himself was going to. "Uh, no, Dad, they're all for me. You'll get yours after dinner."

"Yes," Melody agreed. "I made them for Horace. It's part of our game."

Dr. Splattly gave each of his kids a pat on the head. "Well, I'm glad you can play together. Not all siblings get along as well as you two do." He checked his watch. "Well, I'll see you in an hour when my next session's over. Have fun."

"See you, Daddy," Melody said.

"Bye-bye, sweetie. Bye, big guy," their dad said.

"Bye, Dad," Horace said sadly.

Dr. Splattly stepped outside to walk around to his office, leaving Melody and Horace alone.

Melody took the plate from Horace and led him into the family room. She set the cupcakes and juice on the table. "Have you decided which one it's going to be yet?" she asked.

"I'm not really hungry," Horace said, taking a seat.

"You have to eat at least one," Melody explained. "I need to know if they work."

"If they work?" Horace asked. "What are they supposed to do?"

"Just eat one. I would myself, but I'm the scientist, and everyone knows a scientist must

have a subject upon which she can test her experiments. Now, which will it be?" Melody asked.

"They all look so good, I can't decide," Horace said.

Melody poked her brother's chest. "Do you want me to decide for you?"

Horace gulped.

Melody leaned in closer to Horace's face, so close that he could smell the cucumber-and-cream-cheese sandwich she'd eaten for lunch.

"Of course, the other option is I tie you up and force all four of the cupcakes into your mouth." She backed away from her brother, picked up the plate, and held it out to him. "Decide," she commanded as sweetly as any command could be made. "Eeny, meeny, miney, or mo?"

Horace stared long and hard at the four cupcakes. The black coal cupcake, the gray pebble cupcake, the spiky white cupcake, or the crawling worm cupcake? He thought about it, and decided he'd rather have his sister punch him in the eye or tie him up. He shook his head. "Nope, I'm not eating any. I just can't do it." He shrugged and stared, waiting for her to yell at him.

She didn't. Melody just dropped her chin to her chest, stuck out her bottom lip, and began to cry. Tears rolled out of her eyes and down her cheeks. "I don't understand why you're always so mean to me," she said, her mouth hanging open as she sobbed. "I tried so hard to make these and you won't even taste one." Melody pressed her face into a pillow and began crying louder and louder. "Why are you so horrible? You must hate me!" She sobbed, "That's it! You hate me!"

Horace had seen his sister cry when the light-bulb went out in her Lily Deaver oven and she couldn't bake for a whole afternoon until their mom came home with a new one. Horace had seen his sister cry last year at the Blootinville Talent Pageant when Melody had sung "The Wheels on the Bus" and tap-danced, but then Penny Honey won first place by juggling three live iguanas while riding her pony through a hoop of fire.

But this was the most upset he'd ever seen his sister. He'd watched her spend hours and hours on this cupcake project, and here he was being a mean brother and not even helping her out with her experiment. Horace knew there was no way the cupcakes could *really* kill him, so what was the big deal? All he had to do was take one bite, and if he didn't like it, he could spit it back out. No big deal, Horace decided. And maybe he'd get lucky and the cupcake would taste good.

"Okay, I'm sorry," Horace said, rubbing his sister's back. "I'll try one."

Melody sat up and wiped her puffy red eyes. She sniffled. "You have to eat it all or halves of two different ones," she said, hanging her head sadly. "Please, Horace," she begged. "Please?"

Horace looked at the black coal cupcake. It looked the most harmless and kind of like a normal cupcake. That was possible, wasn't it? "Okay, I'll try this one to start." He picked up the cupcake, raised it to his mouth, and took a small bite from its side.

LET HIM EAT CUPCAKE

The first thing Horace noticed was the cupcake was warm and seemed to become hotter the longer it sat in his mouth. The second thing he noticed was the taste. The icing wasn't sweet like chocolate but tasted like the charcoal briquettes his dad used in the barbecue. The cake wasn't spongy and moist, but dry and splintery.

"Take one big bite and make sure you get some of the jelly filling in the center," Melody ordered.

Jelly filling didn't sound bad at all, Horace thought, so he quickly swallowed the first bite, then opened his mouth as wide as he could. He stuck half the cake past his lips, then bit down sharply. The cupcake crunched between his teeth and fell to the side of his mouth. And then he felt it. A gooey jelly lay on his tongue. Not grape or raspberry or orange marmalade. No, this jelly was like fire burning his tongue. His mouth began heating like a furnace. His tongue felt like it was swelling up to the size of an inflatable raft. Horace's eyes watered. He stood frozen in place, unable to move because of the burning pain in his mouth.

"Drink! Drink!" Melody yelled in his face.

The burning in his mouth blinded Horace. He could feel nothing but his body growing hot-

ter and hotter, as if a ball of fire had exploded inside him and was climbing through his arms, legs, fingers, toes, and brain.

Melody pushed Horace back onto the couch, pulled his mouth open, and poured in the glass of juice. "Drink and swallow," she instructed. "Drink and swallow." She clamped Horace's mouth shut.

Horace felt the liquid cool his tongue. He did as Melody said, chewing and swallowing, chewing and swallowing, until his mouth was empty, his eyes stopped tearing, and he could see again. The heat he felt in his body slowly faded and he soon felt like his normal self, only a little tingly and warm. It wasn't so bad once the burning stopped.

"How do you feel?" Melody asked. She'd taken a Lily Deaver miniature notebook and pen from her apron pocket and wrote her observations.

Horace took a deep breath and put a hand to his forehead, then looked down at his clothes.

"There's—there's no sweat on me or my clothes," he said. He shook his head in disbelief. "How could I be so burning hot and not sweat at all?"

Melody made a note on her pad of paper. "Exactly as I thought. Inner warmth, but cool exterior."

Horace knelt on the carpet and picked up the other half of the cupcake, carefully placing it back on the plate. "Half of that one's enough, I think."

Melody pointed to the plate with her pen. "Which one will you eat next? You said you'd eat two halves."

"I did?" Horace asked, hoping to get out of it.

"Yes, you did," Melody answered.

Horace stared at the plate. "Uh . . . then which one do you think tastes best?"

Melody smiled slyly. "They all taste exactly as they're supposed to."

Horace ran his tongue across his teeth. He'd tried the black one and that had been hot and painful, so maybe if he went in the opposite direction and tried the white one . . . He reached and picked up the white cupcake, holding it up to his face and inspecting it closely. The tiny pointy things on top were the scary part. They looked like pins that were made of ice. He lifted a finger to touch it to the top of the spiky cupcake.

"Uh-uh-uh," Melody said. "You mustn't ruin the decoration."

"I have to know whether they'll cut my mouth, don't I?" he asked.

Melody tapped her pen to her pad of paper. "Horace, you're my only brother and the subject of all my experiments. I would never do anything to harm you. If I did, I'd have no one around to use. I promise that after you eat one more half, if you don't like it, you don't have to do anything I ask ever again."

Horace thought about Melody's deal. If he ate only *one* more half cupcake and didn't like it, Melody would never tie him up and put worms in his hair, she'd never spread spinach paste all over his body, and she'd never dress him like a baby bunny on Easter and make him sit in a large straw basket on the front lawn.

How could he refuse an offer like that?

"Deal," Horace said, and he took the white cupcake, broke it in two, and crammed half of it into his mouth, stuffing his cheeks.

He felt the spiky things prick his gums, his inner cheeks, and the roof of his mouth. The spikes didn't break off. They started growing. The tiny pinlike things pierced his mouth, then continuing to grow and grow, sliding under Horace's skin, then zipping and running through him, covering his face, then wrapping around the back of his head, and down and around his neck and body. They slithered and snaked around his arms and fingers. They wove and wormed their way down his legs, binding his feet and toes. He tried to lift an arm, and he couldn't. He tried to take a step, but his leg wouldn't listen to what his mind was telling it. He tried to open his mouth to yell at his sister, but he couldn't part his lips to speak. But he could move his tongue. Besides his eyes, it was the only part of him he *could* move, and it was then that Horace noticed that although he'd never chewed or swallowed the cupcake, it was completely gone.

Melody stared into his eyes.

"Mmmm-jmmmm-hrmmmm," Horace said through his closed mouth. "Hmmmmrmm-dmmmm-srmmm."

Melody tapped the tip of her pen to Horace's nose. "Can you feel that?" she asked in the same voice a doctor uses when he pokes you with a finger.

Horace shot his eyes to the right, then left as if he were shaking his head.

"No," Melody read off his eyes. She tapped the pen to his stomach. "What about here?"

Again Horace shot his eyes back and forth. "Hrrrmmmmm-brmmmm-crmmmm," he said.

Melody scribbled her findings in her note-book. "The answers to your questions are: *One,* this will wear off in three more minutes. *Two*, the little prickly things on the top of the cupcake were just the ends of all these tiny thin strands that made up the entire cupcake. They were designed to pierce your mouth and slither through and bind your body, just as they now have done. As we speak, they are working their way into your little muscles, veins, and bones. Since you're so puny, the process will go much faster than if you were a larger specimen."

Melody walked circles around Horace. He could see her appear off to his right, then walk past him and disappear off to his left.

"Ten seconds," she said.

Horace counted backward in his head. *Tennineeightsevensixfivefourthreetwoone*.

Nothing happened. He'd probably counted too fast.

"*Now*," Melody said, and on her word, Horace collapsed to the floor in a heap.

Chapter 9

THE BLOW AND POINT

Horace lay there for a moment, stunned that he could have been paralyzed and now be back to normal. He shook out his arms and legs, then stood. "Who would ever want to eat such weird desserts?" he asked. "What's the point?"

Melody smiled. "Just you wait," she said, glancing at her watch. "Give it another minute."

"What do you mean?" he asked. "What's going to happen?" He climbed up on the couch and stared at the mantel clock, watching as the second hand swept past the two, three, four, and five. He turned to his sister. "What do you think is going to happen?" He glanced back to the clock. The second hand passed over the six, seven, and eight. He looked at his arms, wiggled his fingers. The second hand climbed past the nine, ten, eleven, then slid to the twelve.

Horace furrowed his brow and looked at his sister. He folded his arms across his chest and smiled. "See, nothing happened," he said, gloating. "Your experiment didn't work."

Melody sneered at her brother, then frowned.

Horace felt a tickle in his throat and coughed. A puff of black smoke drifted from his mouth.

Melody smiled.

"What did you—" Horace asked, but before he could finish his question, he coughed again. More smoke flowed from his mouth. Hoping to make it stop, he took a deep breath in, then exhaled as hard as he could. A burst of flame shot out of his mouth and across the room, nearly burning the portrait of Great-grandma Splattly that hung on the wall.

Horace gasped and clamped his mouth shut.

"Did it hurt when the fire came out?" Melody asked calmly. "It's not supposed to."

Horace had been so surprised by the fire, he hadn't thought about if it had hurt. He opened his mouth and blew out softly. A thin, small flame danced in the air just off his tongue. He stopped blowing, and the flame died down, then disappeared.

"Well?" Melody asked.

Horace walked around the room, puffing out little bursts of fire, enjoying the trick. He blew hard, and a flame roared halfway across the room and hung in the air. He blew very softly and lit a candle sitting on a table. "We could roast marshmallows over my mouth," he said. "Think of that! And it doesn't really hurt at all. It kind of just tickles a little bit, but not even that much." He gazed at the cupcakes on the plate. "You made this happen with those?"

He pointed to the cupcakes with a hand, and as he did, his feet lifted rapidly into the air. Horace shot straight forward, slammed into the wall, then slid to the carpet. Two little puffs of smoke blew out of his nose.

"Try pointing again," Melody instructed.

Horace lifted his hand and pointed one finger to the ceiling. He slowly lifted off the floor and glided into the air until his finger was touching the ceiling. He peered down at Melody. Horace laughed. He couldn't believe how lucky he was to have such a smart sister. And the funniest part was, she'd baked the cupcakes that would allow him to get away from her whenever she wanted to make him do something he didn't want to do. He could just point and fly away!

Horace clapped his feet together, pointed with one finger, and slowly zipped across the ceiling. He then pointed with two fingers, and zipped a bit faster, then three and four fingers, flying faster and faster laps around the room, until he was so dizzy, he had to stop. When he curled all his fingers into a fist, he found he could rest in midair and just hover.

He crossed his legs and sat in the air just out of Melody's reach. He grinned from ear to ear. "Hey, this is pretty great. I guess I like those cupcakes after all."

"Come down here, please," Melody said.

Horace pointed to the ceiling and flew up higher. "First you have to catch me," he hissed, a small flame dancing in the air. "Be careful I don't light you on fire."

Melody plopped down in a chair, looked at her watch, then made an entry in her notebook. She tapped her head, stood, took the plate of

cupcakes, and left the room, heading into the kitchen.

Horace flew after her. "Come back here. Where are you going?" he asked. He flew lower and slower so he wouldn't crash into any of the doorways or break any of the furniture. He entered the kitchen and lowered himself to the floor, watching as Melody wrapped the leftover cupcakes in aluminum foil.

"I was just joking," Horace said. "I would never burn you or anything like that." He went up to her. "Thanks for doing this. It's the greatest. I'm my own superhero."

Melody rolled her eyes. "Horace, you're *my* superhero. *I* own *you*."

Horace pointed and zipped to the ceiling, a smile across his face. "How could that be if I'm the one with the superpowers?"

Melody dropped her wrapped cupcakes into her Lily Deaver tote bag and slung it over her shoulder. "Because I'm the one with the cupcakes and recipes."

"So?" Horace asked.

Melody walked from the room with the air of a queen. "The powers don't last very long, squirt," she told him as she walked upstairs to her room. "If you want to keep them, you're going to have to do whatever I say."

Chapter 10

MELODY'S SUPERHERO?

Horace flew after his sister a bit too fast, tangling himself in the canopy over her Lily Deaver bed. "Whoa!" he called. He thrashed around, his arms and legs twisted in the fabric. After a couple of minutes, he had finally gotten himself untangled. He flew down and sat on the end of the bed. Melody's room and furniture were painted lavender with a row of white-and-pink tulips stenciled along the walls. Next to her desk on the right was her Lily Deaver Spill & Brew Science Laboratory. Next to her desk on the left was her Lily Deaver Stitch & Thread Sewing Machine. Melody unpacked her schoolbooks, sat in her desk chair, and swiveled to the left.

Horace watched his sister pick up a near-finished lavender outfit. "My powers are going to wear off?" he asked. "How long will they stay?"

Melody booted up her Lily Deaver lavender laptop computer, pulled up a file, then returned to her sewing. "About two hours. I can't be exactly sure. This is the first time I've tried this."

Horace pointed a finger and flew over and sat in the air in front of his sister. "Can I have more of the cupcakes so they last longer? I want to show Auggie and Xax."

Melody slammed a hand down on her desk and gave her brother a hard stare. "No one can ever know of this, Horace! If Mom and Dad find out, they'll take away all my Lily Deaver equipment. Then I'll never be able to make more cupcakes. And don't even think about trying to steal the leftovers. Each cupcake has different powers, and if I'm not there to supervise, who knows what could happen?"

Horace scowled. "Then what's the fun of this for me?"

Melody shook her head. "It's not supposed

to be fun. This is serious business. I need you to fly over to Penny Honey's house and spy on her historical diorama project. Then we'll decide if I need you to destroy it."

Horace went bug-eyed. "Are you crazy? I can't do that. Anyone outside would see me."

Melody held up the shiny pale purple fabric. "Can't you see what I'm doing?" she asked. "I'm making you a costume. You'll be able to go any-where and do anything I tell you."

"A purple costume! I thought that was one of your dresses!" he cried. He slapped his hands to his head, dropped to the floor, then knelt on the carpet so his chin rested on the edge of the sewing table. "Why can't it be a cool color like blue or black like Superman or Batman wear? Not pale purple like a petunia!" he exclaimed.

Melody pointed her scissors at her brother's nose. "Do you enjoy the powers I gave you? Do you want to keep having them and try new ones?"

Horace nodded. "Yes, but—"

"Then you're going to wear what I tell you," Melody interrupted. She took her Lily Deaver measuring tape and wrapped it around Horace's head. She made a note of the measurement on her computer, then continued sewing. "Now that I think of it, a superhero does have to have a name, too. Hmmm . . . what should we call you?"

Horace stood and smiled. "How about Captain Incredible or Meteorman?" he asked.

Melody shook her head. "No-no-no. Your name needs to be special. Like nothing anyone's ever heard before."

"I'm thinking," Horace said. He put his fingers to his chin and ear in his thinking pose. "And what I'm thinking is that since my powers will change because of the different kinds of cupcakes, how about I'm called Chameleonman, named after the lizard that can change its colors."

Melody stood and held up the finished costume. "Try this on while I cut out the letters to stick your name across the back," she directed.

Horace frowned at the outfit. "Are you sure I have to be purple?" he asked glumly.

Melody reached into her fabric box and pulled out a piece of pink lace. "Say one more word about it and I'll add this to the wings."

• • •

Horace went to his room, clutching the purple costume in a fist. He couldn't believe it! Here he was with superhero powers, and not only did his sister have total control of the cupcakes, but she was making him wear a costume that was the color of flowers!

Horace slumped on his bed. He couldn't even show off to his friends without the costume. If he did, his parents would hear about it and say the cupcakes were too dangerous. Then he'd *never* get to fly or breathe fire again. Horace took a deep breath and exhaled a flame. He pointed his finger and did circles and loops around his room.

Horace knew what he had to do. He picked

the costume up off the bed. It was better to be a purple superhero than to be no superhero at all.

He slipped on the outfit and was covered from head to toe and fingertip to fingertip in pale purple taffeta. The material was smooth and hugged his body tight. Under each arm was a large birdlike wing that attached to the body of the suit. When Horace lifted his arms up and down, the wings unfurled and made a rustling noise. Around his neck was a cape attached to a large collar that stood straight up as high as his ears. Covering his head was a tight hood that came down over his face, ending at the tip of his nose. Holes were cut in the hood for his ears and eyes. He stood before his bedroom mirror. The costume fit perfectly, he had to admit, and if it hadn't been purple, he'd have loved it.

He returned to Melody's room to find her applying glue to a bunch of letters on her desk. She looked at her brother and patted her computer proudly. "I had most of your measurements on my laptop from last Halloween when I

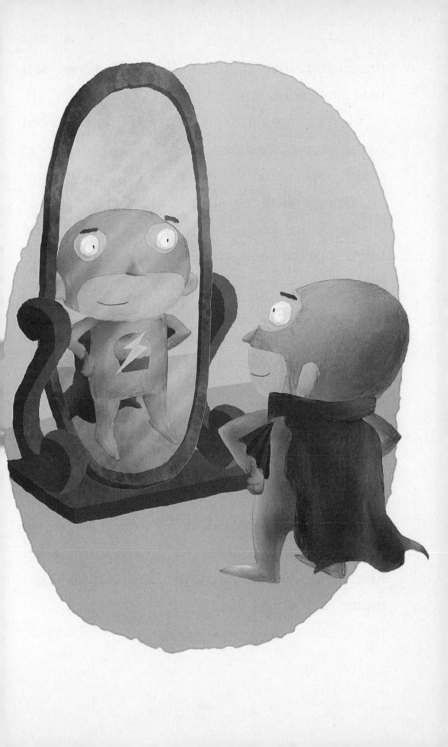

made you that parrot costume. I guess you haven't grown a bit."

Horace fought back a frown and walked around his sister to the desk. "So I'm going to be Chameleon-man?" he asked.

Melody pointed.

Lying facedown across the desktop were the bright orange letters his sister had cut out with their gluey sides facing up, waiting to be stuck on the costume.

Melody gathered the cutouts off the desk and spun Horace around. She immediately began slapping the gluey sides to his back.

"Hey, wait a minute!" Horace yelled.

Melody stuck the last of the letters to Horace's costume. "There we go. *Absolutely lovely,*" she remarked.

"Lovely?" Horace asked. He turned and stood backward before Melody's closet mirror. He twisted his head around, peeking over the costume's high collar. *"OH NO!!!"* he cried.

THE CUPCAKED CRUSADER

"The Cupcaked Crusader!" Horace shouted. "That's . . . that's babyish!"

"That's what makes it so special," Melody replied. "No one will ever suspect that the Cupcaked Crusader could be a spy. And since you're about the size of a cupcake, it suits you." She turned Horace to face her. "Now you know what to do, right?"

"Yeah, the Cupcaked Crusader knows what to do," he moaned. "Follow his sister's orders."

Melody lifted one of Horace's arms and pulled at the wing. "Did you notice the secret pockets I put in?" She pulled a tiny zipper that was sewn in under the wing. "If I need you to, you can hide stuff in here."

Horace took his arm back. "Nothing too heavy or I might not be able to fly," he said.

"Hey, kids, how are you doing up there?" Dr. Splattly called from the living room.

Melody wagged a finger in Horace's face. "Don't even think about pulling any stunts," she whispered, then she yelled out the door: "We're fine, Dad. Horace is helping me with my history diorama."

"Glad to hear it," he shouted up the stairs. "Okay, kids. See you in another hour."

Horace and Melody heard the door close. Melody took her brother's arm and walked him downstairs to the back door. "Now pay very close attention to everything you see Penny do. Then report back to me and we'll figure out our next step." She opened the door. "Always take off and fly from the backyard behind the gardening shed, okay? That way no one will see you. And don't worry if you're late getting back. When Dad checks on us, I'll tell him you're busy taking one of my soothing peanut butter and horseradish baths and can't be bothered."

Horace slowly began walking across the yard. Always to be ordered around by his little sister! He couldn't stand it anymore! He was the older kid in this family! He should be in charge!

"And Horace?" Melody said.

He turned just before the shed. "Yeah, what?" he asked angrily.

Melody grinned a bossy, mean grin. "You make a great Cupcaked Crusader." She laughed gleefully.

Horace stomped off behind the shed. He raised both his hands as high as he could, pointed with all his fingers, and rocketed into the sky. He zigzagged between the clouds. How *dare* she decide everything for him!

Then Horace peered down at Blootinville. *Yowee-zowee-zooks!* He couldn't believe it! He could see the entire town, from Rumbly Mountain in the north to the dump and airport in the south, from the Chef Nibbles Canned Food factory in the east to the Happy Acres

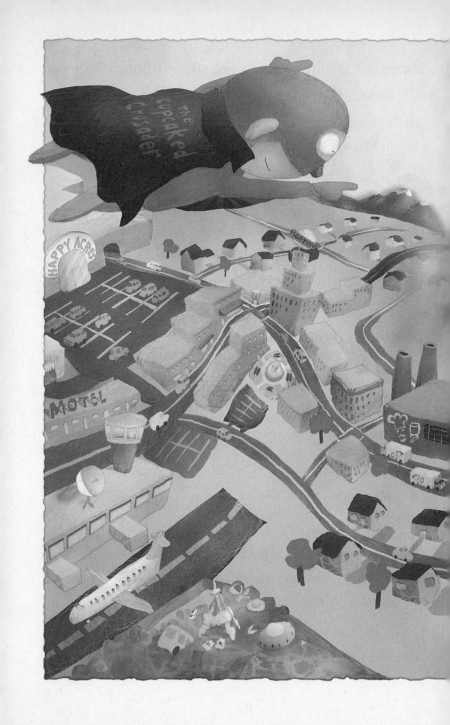

Shopping Mall in the west. The houses were as small as his thumbnail. The cars looked like colorful jelly beans gliding along the roads. The people were tiny like specks drawn with a pencil tip. When they moved, it was like they were scribbles on paper.

Horace pointed and curled three fingers on each hand, dipping lower in the sky. He flew just above the rooftops of the houses. He watched families bringing groceries in from their cars and kids playing soccer, baseball, and Blootinball in their backyards. He saw a policeman riding a horse down a street.

Penny Honey's big yellow house was just ahead of him. He flew over its high roof and closed his hand, sitting in the air just above its chimney. Horace thought long and hard, then longer and harder. Sure, he could do what his sister ordered and then go directly home, but what would be the fun in that? What was the fun of having superpowers if he just did what she said? Did other superheroes take orders from their little sisters? Did other superheroes get picked on by bullies and science teachers?

Horace thought not.

Horace Splattly would be in charge from now on! Horace Splattly would call all the shots!

At least while he was the Cupcaked Crusader.

He raised his hands and zipped into the sky, flying out of his neighborhood and into the town center with its tall buildings and busy streets. The tallest building in town belonged to the *Blootinville Banner*, where his mom worked. Horace and his sister had been to his mother's office on the forty-third floor many times. Mari Splattly took her kids to work with her some Saturdays. Horace and Melody had their own articles on the Kids Page of the Sunday paper. "Melody Presents . . ." was a column filled with recipes, home decorating tips, and advice about how to be the perfect tea-party hostess or inventor. Each week Horace wrote stories about a family of aliens who lived deep inside Rumbly Mountain. Horace thought it could be true, but his mother always put his stories under the headline IMAGINE THAT!

Horace flew up the side of the building and peered inside the window of his mother's office. His mom sat behind her desk with her back to the window, talking on the phone. Horace rapped a fist against the glass, making a sharp *pangy* noise.

Mrs. Splattly spun her chair to look out the window. Her eyes went wide. She dropped the phone and picked up a pen and pad of paper. "What are you?" she called through the glass.

Horace laughed, blew out a large burst of fire, then blasted away. He couldn't wait to hear what she said about a flying, fire-breathing purple superhero when she got home!

A Dear Miss (and a Near Miss)

Beyond the town center stood a cluster of apartment buildings. Many of the apartments had balconies where people relaxed, read, napped, or just enjoyed the view of the Blootinville skyline. Horace flew past, waving to people as he did somersaults, back flips, and twists. He soared up high, then took a steep plunge. He nose-dived to the earth as if he were going to crash into the ground. At the last second, he rocketed skyward and breathed a stream of fire into the air.

Men and women, boys and girls stood on their balconies and applauded.

"Who are you?" a man asked.

"Where did you come from?" a woman wondered.

A man snapped a picture of Horace. "Tell us your name."

Horace spun around and showed them his back. He was afraid to say the name out loud in case someone made fun of him.

"'The Cupcaked Crusader'?" a woman said, reading the name on the costume.

"What's a cupcake-crusader, Daddy?" a little boy asked.

"I'm not sure, but I think we just saw our first one," the boy's father replied.

Horace soared into the sky, a wide smile across his face. He may have had a stupid name, but he was still a superhero.

• • •

Horace flew over the rolling countryside of Blootinville. People of all ages pointed and called and waved. Horace was enjoying his flight around town. At the bottom of a hill, he spotted a sight that delighted his eyes. There, on the sidewalk, was Sara Willow. She had changed from her school clothes into pink-and-white-striped overalls and pink-and-white-striped sneakers. Sara had a pair of headphones over her ears, and she skipped rope while singing quietly. Her eyes were shut, and she was gently rocking her head back and forth to the music.

Horace thought she had to be the prettiest girl in all of Blootinville.

Just then, Horace heard a squeaking noise. He looked to the top of the hill. A small child had just gotten off his red tricycle, but instead of holding on to it, he had let it go. Now the vehicle was rolling down the sidewalk, picking up speed as it went.

Squeak, squeak, squeak, the tires shrieked.

"My trikey-bike," the little boy cried.

Horace saw that the runaway tricycle was aimed directly at Sara. If she didn't get out of the way fast, it would mow her down.

"Young miss, please move out of the way," Horace called in a low voice.

With her headphones on, Sara couldn't hear him or the tricycle. She just kept skipping rope and singing to herself.

The tricycle sped wildly down the hill. Horace knew what he had to do. If he didn't act quickly, the tricycle would crush Sara to the pavement.

Horace raised all his fingers and sped through the air like a bullet. He swooped down and swept Sara into his arms and off the sidewalk. He lifted her into the air just as the speeding tricycle whipped past and careened into the Willow family mailbox, knocking it to the ground.

Sara thrashed around in Horace's arms, trying to get free. "What are you doing?" she yelled. "Put me down!" She struck Horace on the head with a jump-rope handle.

Horace flew Sara to her front yard and set her on her feet. She immediately flung her jump rope at him, tangling Horace's legs in the cord.

"Who are you?" Sara asked. "What do you think you're doing?" she screamed.

Horace lowered his voice to sound older. "I was saving you from that dangerous machine," he said, and pointed to the tricycle. "It was

headed straight for you." Horace stepped out of the jump rope, picked it up, and handed it back to Sara.

Sara took it and looked at the tricycle and the broken mailbox. She then fixed her gaze on this mysterious superhero. "You saved me?" she asked. "Oh. I thought . . . I didn't know what was happening. I was scared and . . ." She stopped talking as a tear slid down her cheek.

"You're safe now, miss," Horace told Sara. "You don't have to cry."

"Who—who are you?" Sara asked.

He turned so she could read his back.

"'The Cupcaked Crusader'?" she asked, a smile growing across her face. "I was saved by a cupcake. How funny."

"No!" Horace declared, stomping a foot to the ground. "Not a *cupcake*. A superhero."

Sara laughed. "Well, you're the smallest superhero I've ever seen."

Horace frowned.

"But also the cutest," Sara said. "I wasn't trying to be mean." She walked to Horace, leaned down, and gave him a kiss on the cheek. "Thanks for saving me, Cupcaked Crusader."

Horace got all tingly, and he blushed a bright red. "Uh, gee, you're welcome," he said as he took a quick look down the street to make sure no one had seen Sara kiss him. "I guess I, uh, should be going to save other people now. Uh, see you in school tomorrow, Sara."

Horace lifted his hands and flew off into the sky.

Sara stared up at her new hero. "You'll see me in *school* tomorrow?" she asked. "How do you know my name?"

Chapter 13

THE DRAGON OF BLOOTIN MANOR

Horace didn't answer Sara. He kept right on flying without looking back.

How could he have been so stupid? He'd almost given away who he was to her. If he didn't keep his identity a secret, he wouldn't get any more cupcakes. Sure, Sara thought he was the cutest when he was a superhero with powers, but without them, what would she think?

Horace flew between houses and glided around trees. How long would these powers last? He hadn't been keeping track of time and wasn't sure when he'd stop flying and breathing fire. Would the flying stop slowly so he'd gradually float to the ground? Or would it stop all at once, sending him falling to the earth like a rock?

Horace spied Blootin Manor at the top of Society Hill and got an idea. He would just have to play a prank on Auggie and Xax.

How could he not?

The Blootins had one of the largest and oldest homes in Blootinville, dating back over one hundred years. It was a large stone house with a black slate roof that peaked to a point. Eight stone chimneys sprang from the roof at different angles. In one arm of the U-shaped house, the maids, butlers, gardeners, chefs, and chauffeurs slept. Mayor A. X. Blootin, Mrs. Serena Blootin, and Auggie and Xax lived in the other parts. Hedges of red, yellow, white, purple, pink, and black roses stood six feet tall and made a maze that ran throughout the yard. If a person wasn't careful, he could get lost in it for hours or even days. When Auggie and Xax played in the maze, they carried cell phones so if they got lost, they could phone a gardener to come find them.

Horace flew over the maze and up to the front of the house. He located Auggie's window and flew up to the glass. No Auggie in sight. Horace flew three windows down to Xax's room and peered in through the glass.

The two brothers sat on Xax's bed, playing a video game. Mitsy, Mrs. Blootin's large blue poodle, lay on the floor, sleeping. Horace glanced across the room to the empty fireplace. *Perfect*. He flew up to the roof and landed on the slate shingles, gripping the edge of the stone chimney that led to the fireplace in Xax's room. He leaned his head over the dark opening, took a deep breath, and blew.

A large flame shot from Horace's mouth and down the chimney.

Horace stopped blowing and listened.

"A dragon! The dragon of Blootin Manor's on the roof!" one of the twins screamed.

Horace blew another blast of fire down the chimney. *"Arrrrrrrrrrr!"* he roared.

"It's Gretel!" one of the twins shouted.

Horace flew down to the window and watched as the twins cowered on the bed, each clutching a pillow and staring at the fireplace as they waited for the demon monster to come down into the room. Mitsy dashed back and forth, barking loudly.

Horace rapped his knuckles on the window. When Auggie and Xax turned to look, Horace blew a burst of fire into the air. "Rrrr-arrrrrrrgh!" he moaned.

Mitsy ran to the window and barked.

"The dragon's come for us!" Xax shrieked, pulling his bedcovers up over his head.

Horace watched as Auggie grabbed a metal ruler and thick book off Xax's desk. Using the ruler as a sword and the book as a shield, he slowly approached the window. "For the sake of the manor, we must defeat it," he told his brother. "Mitsy, prepare to attack."

"Don't do it!" Xax yelled. "I'll call nine-one-one." He grabbed for the phone on his nightstand.

Auggie pushed up the window and struck out with the ruler. "Stay back, you monster," he shouted at Horace. "What say you? Why have you come here?"

Mitsy snarled at the purple monster, baring her teeth.

Horace grinned at his friend and waved a friendly hand. "Hey, Auggie. Hey, Xax," he called. He flew through the window, over Auggie and Mitsy, and into the room. Horace stood on the carpet and exhaled a puff of smoke. "What's going on with you guys?"

Mitsy trotted up to the purple thing and sniffed.

"It's a little purple dragon," Xax called to his brother. "Be careful. I think it's Gretel's son. I'll phone the fire department while you kill him, okay?"

Horace reached up and gave Mitsy's head a pat. The dog yipped, wagging her tail fast. She gave Horace a big tongue smack on his face. "Hey, Mitsy." Horace laughed. He peeled the hood back from his face.

Auggie tossed down the book and ruler and stared at the creature that had entered the Blootin home.

Xax set down the phone, dropped the bed-covers, and leaned forward. He took a long, careful look at what he had thought was a dangerous monster. "Horace Splattly, have you turned into a little purple dragon?"

"Whoa, man! What's happened to you?" Auggie asked.

Xax scrambled to the foot of the bed and lay on his stomach, staring at his friend. "Do you think maybe you're the *son* of the Dragon of Blootin Manor? Is it possible you have a crazy half-beast, half-boy thing going on?" he asked.

Horace let out a laugh. "I'm not any part dragon, Xax. I'm all boy, just like I've always been. I was just playing a prank on you guys. My sister made me eat these scary cupcakes. All of a sudden I could fly and breathe fire." He turned in a circle to show them his costume. "Melody's making me wear this so no one will know who I am. I've flown all over town this afternoon. It's great, but the powers will probably wear off soon." Horace grinned mischievously. "I'm supposed to be spying on Penny Honey for my sister, but instead I took off to do what *I* want. She'd kill me if she knew I told you guys what's going on."

Xax looked at his brother. "Do you think he's lying?" he asked. "Maybe the dragon's just *pretending* to be Horace to trick us."

"I swear, I'm not a dragon," Horace said. "Ask me anything about school to prove it."

Xax looked to Auggie. "Go ahead and ask him something."

Auggie stood before Horace. "Okay, who is the kid who gave away the secrets of the *Big Notebook of Worldwide Conspiracies* today?"

Horace hung his head and pointed to himself. "Okay, it's me. Horace Splattly. Sorry, guys."

Auggie nodded to Xax and Xax nodded to Auggie. "You're forgiven," both brothers said to Horace.

Auggie smiled and stepped forward, shaking

his friend's hand. "Wow, Horace, I can't believe this is you."

"One-three-five-seven!" Xax exclaimed. "When I saw that fire come down the chimney, I was so scared I lost track of how many times I blinked this afternoon."

"Those must be some wild cupcakes," Auggie said, inspecting Horace's costume. "Do you think there's any way you could get the recipe so we could try them?"

"I'd really love to fly over to Principal Nosair's house and see what he does after school," Xax said. "Ryan Bryans told me he saw Nosair Hula-Hooping in his driveway dressed like a panda bear."

Horace flew up and sat on the corner of the fireplace mantel, for once looking down at the twins instead of up at them. "I don't know if the recipe's written down. It might just be in Melody's head. And she's protecting the cup-cakes so I can't take them."

"Have you done anything cool?" Xax asked

"What have you seen?"

Horace told the boys about flying to the town center, seeing his mother, and saving Sara from the runaway tricycle.

"That's it?" Auggie said.

Horace frowned. "Yeah, so far. Why? What am I supposed to be doing?"

Auggie shrugged. "I don't know, but none of that sounds like real superhero stuff. Does it, Xax?"

Xax sat up in bed. "Nah, not really. It does sound like fun, but still, it's not too exciting by the standards of most superheroes."

Horace flew around the room in a circle. "Hmmm . . . I am thinking about what you said, and what I'm thinking is that you're right. If I am going to be a superhero, I should do something really superheroic like fight evil villains and stuff." He flew down face-to-face with Auggie and Xax. "Is that what you mean?"

Xax nodded. "Uh-huh."

Auggie nodded. "That would be the totally coolest."

Horace landed on the floor and stepped across the room to the window. He gazed at the sun as it set over Blootinville. Horace looked at the town, the canned-food factory, Kitty Meloise's Don't Be Ugly Beauty Salon, and the Food-to-Eat Supermarket. When he looked to his left, he saw Blootinville Elementary and the school yard.

The sun was setting on the Blootinville Elementary school yard. Horace remembered what he'd seen yesterday. He remembered what Chef Quaquaqua had told his father this afternoon.

Xax and Auggie stood on either side of Horace.

"Hey, guy, what are you thinking?" Auggie asked.

"It's getting dark out there," Xax said. "Shouldn't you be heading home?"

Horace smiled from ear to ear. "It's monster time," he replied.

Chapter 14

A MONSTER MISSION

"Monster time?" Xax asked.

"You can't mean what I think you mean," Auggie said. "No way, man."

Horace marched over to Xax's shelves and picked up a camera. "I'm going to need to borrow this for tonight, okay?"

Xax grabbed Horace's arm. "You can't go do this. It's too dangerous."

"What if you're right and there really is a monster on the playground?" Auggie asked.

Horace nodded and looped the camera strap over a shoulder. "That's exactly what we need to find out," he explained. "Don't you want to know if it exists?"

"Of course," Auggie answered. "But—"

"Well, now we can know," Horace interrupted. "I can *fly* over the yard, watch for him, take a picture, and see who's taming him and why. I won't even have to set my feet on the ground, so I'll be perfectly safe. Tomorrow we'll be able to show everyone the photo, and they won't think we're dorky anymore."

Auggie and Xax looked at each other, then back to Horace.

"You promise you'll only fly over the school and then head straight home?" Auggie asked.

Horace nodded. "I promise," he said.

Xax dropped his head into his hands, his hair falling over his face. "This has to be the craziest thing that's ever happened," he said.

Horace gave him a pat on the back. "Don't worry, I'll give your camera back tomorrow."

Xax looked up. "I'm not worried about the camera. I'm worried about the monster and its evil trainer."

The phone rang. A moment later, Mrs. Blootin yelled down the hall, "Xax! Auggie! It's

Melody Splattly calling. She wants to know if you've seen Horace this afternoon. Can you pick up the phone?"

Horace pulled his hood over his head. "You've got to keep it a secret that I told you, or Melody will never let me have the cupcakes again," he whispered. "Just think of how many conspiracies we might be able to prove if I have more powers."

Mrs. Splattly yelled down the hall, "Boys, Melody's waiting to talk to you."

"Okay, guys?" Horace asked.

Auggie nodded. "Okay, I promise to keep it a secret."

Xax nodded. "Done." He reached for the phone.

Mitsy gave Horace a good-luck good-bye lick on the cheek.

Horace strode to the window and raised his arms. "Bye, guys, I'm outta here." And just as the sun set behind Blootinville Elementary School, Horace took off into the evening sky.

• • •

The sky was a dark blue and twinkled with the light of millions of stars. A full moon glowed brightly, lighting Horace's way. He flew over the town of Blootinville, watching as moms and dads called their kids inside to eat their suppers. Horace flew by the large clock on the library in the town square and saw that it was 6:14. His dad would be checking on him and Melody again in thirty-six minutes. His mom would be home from the paper at just about the same time. Horace hoped the monster was already out on the playground so he could just snap a picture, fly by Penny Honey's window, and then return home.

He passed the Lickety-Split Car Wash, the All-You-Can-Chew Hot Dog Hut, and took a right turn. There before him was Blootinville Elementary. The building was dark and silent, all the kids safe at home. Horace passed over the school's roof and saw three red rubber balls, two Frisbees, five dirty sneakers, fourteen pairs of underwear, and one Lily Deaver Fly-Right Transformer Jet Plane & Egg Beater, which his sister had lost one recess when she'd tossed it too high.

He took a dive and grabbed his sister's toy from the roof, zipping it into a pocket under a wing. He sailed over the school yard, flying high enough to keep a safe distance between himself and the ground. He flew over the jungle gym, seesaws, four-square blacktop, and baseball diamond, then stopped dead in the air. Horace's jaw dropped. He was staring so hard he felt like his eyes would pop out of his head.

There on the playground stood the humongous hairy monster he had seen last night!

The monster was the size of a bus and shaped like a loaf of bread. In the dim light, Horace could see that it was covered with long brown, white, and black hair that drooped over its body and spread across the ground, covering its feet. The monster began creeping across the playground. It moved slowly, as if the weight of

its huge body were too heavy to carry on its legs.

Horace trembled with excitement. He lifted the camera from his side and adjusted the settings. He held it to an eye and aimed at the hairy beast.

Click, the shutter snapped.

Horace had his picture.

He was about to take a second photo when the thought hit him. *Chipper!* The monster looked exactly like a giant-sized Chipper!

Horace remembered the tomato plant from

science class. First there was the puny one, then the large one that Mr. Dienow had treated with chemicals. Could Dienow have done the same thing to the guinea pig?

Just then the wind picked up, blowing Horace off balance. He flew backward, dropping the camera. For a moment, it hung from the camera strap over his shoulder, but then the camera strap slid down his arm and the camera fell to the ground. He looked down to see it drop to a soft patch of grass by the swing set.

Yes, he had promised his friends he would not set a foot on the ground and only fly above the school, but how could he ever tell them he saw the monster, took a photograph that proved it existed, then lost the camera?

No way was that going to happen.

Horace looked across the yard and saw that the giant guinea pig was pretty far from where the camera had fallen. That would give him plenty of time to fly down, snatch it up, and take off into the sky.

How could there be a problem with that?

Horace dropped to the ground and stood on the grass. He looked down, but couldn't see the camera. "I know it was just here," he said to himself.

"Hello, flying creature. What are you doing at my school?"

Horace glanced up to see Principal Nosair standing above him, holding Xax's camera.

"I'm the Cupcaked Crusader. A superhero. Thanks for finding that for me," Horace said, holding out a hand.

The principal nodded and glanced at the camera. It was labeled with a piece of tape that read: *Xax Blootin*. He looked down at Horace with a serious expression. "Where did you find this?" he asked.

Behind the principal, Horace could see Chipper creeping toward them. His mouth was open, and his large teeth were bared.

"I think we should get out of here, sir," Horace said.

"I'm beginning to think you're up to mischief," Nosair said. "Maybe we should go to my office and have a chat."

Chipper crawled closer, snapping his mouth open and closed, only a few feet behind the principal.

"Sir," Horace pleaded. "You've got to get out of here. A giant guinea pig is coming, and I think he wants to eat you."

The principal stared hard at Horace. "That's enough of your foolishness, young creature. Let's head to my office."

"I'm not kidding," Horace said, his voice louder, more scared.

Nosair pulled at Horace to take him into the school. Chipper was right behind the principal, only a couple of yards away. "I'm warning you," Horace said. He lifted his arms and took off into the air just as Chipper was about to pounce.

"You're not going anywhere," Nosair commanded, and he grabbed hold of Horace's foot, keeping him from flying higher.

Chapter 15

IN THE BELLY OF THE BEAST

*G*lomp!

Chipper opened his mouth and closed it over Principal Nosair, sucking him in. The only part of the principal not inside Chipper was his arm. His hand was still holding tight to Horace's ankle as Horace tried to fly away. Chipper's beady black eyes looked fierce with anger.

"Help! Oh my! Help me get out of here!"

Chipper opened his mouth again to suck in the rest of Nosair.

Horace kicked his other foot at Nosair's fingers and was able to get free. Just as Chipper swallowed the last of the principal, Horace flew to safety. He looked down at the school yard. Chipper stood, looking up at him. Across the yard, he saw a man step out of the woods and into the moonlight.

Mr. Dienow.

Dienow began walking across the playground to the oversized class pet.

"Help! I can't breathe!" the principal called from inside Chipper.

Horace flew down in front of Chipper's huge face. Chipper opened his mouth and snapped.

"Hey, stay away!" Dienow called.

"Help! Help!" the principal yelled from inside the guinea pig.

Horace flew higher, out of Mr. Dienow's reach. "Why have you created this giant guinea pig?"

Mr. Dienow grinned. "What are you? Some kind of mutant insect?" He laughed and grabbed for Horace. "Maybe I should pull off one of your little wings."

"I'm the Cupcaked Crusader, and I'm here to save Principal Nosair," Horace answered.

"Oh, no you're not, you little flying freak." Dienow sneered. "I've spent years waiting to get rid of my brother. No purple runt is going to stop me."

"You planned to have this giant guinea pig attack him?" Horace asked.

Dienow laughed. "I invited my brother out here to see my new experiment, then hid and let my pet attack him." He tapped a finger to his watch. "By the way, if you plan to save him, you'd better hurry. In three minutes, my brother will be guinea-pig food and I'll take over the school, then Blootinville, and then the world."

"You want to hurt your older brother?" Horace asked. He thought of the many experiments Melody had performed on him. Did all younger siblings want to torture their older brothers?

"I won't miss him," Dienow replied. "Time's ticking, insect. Better do some quick saving."

Chipper opened his mouth wide.

Horace knew what he had to do. He pointed his fingers, took a deep breath, and flew inside Chipper's mouth and down his throat.

Chipper's insides were moist and hot and smelled like rotten lettuce. Horace dived into the guinea pig's stomach. It was a large, dark room shaped like a dented oval. Horace set his feet down on the sticky stomach floor and breathed a small fire to light the room. Principal Nosair lay facedown in the corner in a pile of chewed-up celernip. Horace flew over and shook him awake. They only had a couple of minutes to escape before they both were digested.

The principal opened his eyes and pulled away from Horace. "What's going on?" he asked.

Horace yanked the principal to his feet. "Come on, we have to get out of here fast." Horace flew into the air, ready to make an escape. Suddenly Chipper began to shake.

"Oh my, what's happening?" the principal asked. "Is it an earthquake?"

The guinea pig's stomach began growing smaller around them. Horace remembered the tomato plant from the classroom and how it looked smaller at the end of class than it had at the beginning. Apparently, Dienow's chemicals didn't make things grow big forever, only for a short time. Now Chipper was shrinking just like the tomato plant.

The guinea pig's stomach shrank more, and the top of it hit Principal Nosair's head. Seconds later, Chipper had shrunk so much that Horace didn't have room to fly. The superhero and his principal crawled on their knees through the moist tunnel as it grew smaller and smaller around them.

They reached the end of Chipper's throat, and Horace squeezed out and into his mouth. Nosair followed but got stuck halfway through.

"Help me!" Principal Nosair cried. "The throat's squeezing me tighter and tighter." Horace knelt in Chipper's closed mouth. The animal was quickly shrinking around them. Its large, sharp teeth got closer and closer.

"Pull me out!" the principal cried.

Horace gave a pull on Nosair's arms but

couldn't get the principal free. The throat had closed too tightly around his body. "Hold on," Horace said. He turned around, took a breath, and breathed out a puff of smoke. Chipper coughed a small cough but didn't open his mouth.

"Hurry!" Principal Nosair yelled. "He's trying to suck me back into his stomach."

Horace took the deepest breath he possibly could and exhaled a huge cloud of smoke. It filled the guinea pig's mouth and flowed through his body. Suddenly Chipper began bucking. His mouth opened wide, and he coughed a cough so loud and so hard that Horace and the principal were thrown clear out of the guinea pig and across the playground. They lay in a patch of dirt and quickly turned to see if the large animal was coming for them.

But nothing was there. No guinea pig. No Dienow. Just an empty playground under a star-lit sky. They sat back, breathed in the fresh air, and realized they'd narrowly missed becoming guinea-pig food by only a few seconds.

The principal gasped for air and wiped his hair out of his face. "Whew, that was certainly a close call," he said. "I was supposed to meet my brother here. I guess it's a good thing he didn't show up and you did." He brushed off his suit, stood, and held out his hand. "Thanks for saving me. I guess I won't have to take you into my office now."

Horace stood on the playground and shook the principal's hand. "Glad to hear it, sir. But I'm sorry to say I must warn you that someone sent that monster to get you."

"Sent that monster for *me*?" the principal asked. "Now why would anyone want to hurt me? I'm a friendly guy."

Horace was about to tell him about his brother's evil plan when the principal reached down and gave Horace a pat on the shoulder. "Well, never you mind," he said. "It was just a silly accident that the guinea pig ate me. And with you around to protect the school, I'm sure it will never come back. I'm going to phone the *Blootinville Banner* right now and make sure they know all about you." The principal smiled at Horace. His teeth glinted a bright white in the moonlight. "I'm really sorry about taking that camera. I guess I left it in the monster somewhere." Principal Nosair smiled. "Of course, feel free to visit again if another monster comes around." And then he marched right into the school, leaving Horace alone in the middle of the playground.

With no one left to save, nothing left to do, Horace lifted his arms, pointed his fingers, and waited to fly off into the air.

Nothing happened.

He took a breath and blew.

Not even a puff of smoke. Just as Melody had said, the powers would wear off. Now the Cupcaked Crusader didn't exist at all, and Horace was just a boy in a dumb, purple taffeta superhero outfit. He took off the hooded mask and let it dangle down his back.

How completely humiliating.

No capture of Mr. Dienow.

No camera to return to Xax.

No photo of Chipper as proof that the monster existed.

And tomorrow at school, Sara Willow would talk all about how the Cupcaked Crusader saved her, never knowing that he was really Horace Splattly.

Horace sighed a big sigh.

Being a superhero and keeping a secret identity was a lot harder than he'd thought it would be.

Chapter 16

WHAT SWEET MELODY IS THIS?
PART 2

Horace began walking home.

Before he'd gone a block, Melody ran up to him, waving a large green trash bag and pointing a flashlight in his eyes. "Horace, what are you doing?" his sister shouted. She handed him the bag.

Horace squinted from the light, then looked at the garbage bag. "What's this for?"

Melody rolled her eyes and gave a tug on his arm. "You can't come home wearing that costume, or Mom and Dad will figure out what we've been up to. Honestly, Horace, don't you have a brain?"

Horace held the bag back out to Melody. "You think I'm going to wear a garbage bag?"

Melody gritted her teeth. "I cut a hole in it for your head. Just put this on. It will cover you from your neck to your feet."

Horace glared at his sister. He unfolded the bag and pulled it over his head. The bottom of the bag scraped the sidewalk. None of Horace could be seen but his head. Since there were no holes for his arms, he just kept them at his sides.

Melody smiled at her brother. "Now that's much better," she said.

The siblings strolled down the sidewalk to their home. The night was dark, the air was crisp, and their neighborhood was peaceful and quiet.

"How'd you know I'd be at the school?" Horace asked, hoping Xax and Auggie hadn't told her anything.

Melody pointed the flashlight in his eyes, so he had to squint. "When I made the costume, I planted a computer chip in one of your wings. When you didn't come home, all I had to do was turn on my Lily Deaver home satellite. It told me exactly where you were."

Horace looked away from the flashlight. Why did he have to have such a smart sister? "Well, you were right, Miss Genius."

"I'm just trying to be a nice younger sister and keep an eye out for my brother. There's nothing wrong with that, is there?" Melody asked.

"Yeah, right," Horace replied. "You just wanted to know what Penny Honey was up to with her historical diorama project. Well, forget about it."

"You really didn't go there?" Melody asked, genuinely surprised.

"Nope."

Melody stopped in her tracks, slumping her shoulders. "Not at all?" She pouted.

Horace stopped and turned to his sister. "Not at all. You were being so mean and bossy all afternoon, I just couldn't bring myself to do it. I don't mind eating the cupcakes, even though they taste awful, but I do mind being ordered around like a servant. Maybe if you were nicer to me, it would make it easier for me to be nicer to you. And you shouldn't be spying on Penny Honey anyway. You're smart enough without cheating. How many eight-year-old kids could come up with a recipe for cupcakes that give people superpowers?"

Melody started walking home again with Horace at her side. "I suppose I am smart enough to do it without spying, but it's hard not to be curious," she explained. She looked to her older brother. "Do you really think I'm a genius?" she asked.

Horace sighed a big sigh. "Yeah," he admitted. "I really think you're a genius. *And* annoying and bossy, too. *Really, really, really* annoying and bossy." He reached into his wing pocket and took out the Lily Deaver Fly-Right Transformer Jet Plane & Egg Beater and passed it under the garbage bag to his sister. "Here, I found this for you on the school roof," he told her.

Melody happily took her equipment. "Thank you, thank you," she exclaimed. "I never thought I'd see it again. I guess your not going to Penny Honey's wasn't such a bad thing after all, huh?"

"I guess not," Horace replied.

They walked up the path to their front door.

"So what's for dinner?" Horace asked. "You couldn't have had time to cook much with all that went on this afternoon."

Melody gasped with excitement and put a hand to her cheek. "Oh, a good chef can prepare a meal in minutes. I found the most delightful recipes on the Lily Deaver Web site this afternoon. We're having a hot-dog casserole with a cheesy-doodle sauce and celernip fries."

Horace smiled and shook his head. How did his sister ever do it? She was a pain, but she *was* a brilliant pain. "So are we having cupcakes for dessert?" he asked.

Melody laughed. "Absolutely not! For dessert, I baked miniature-green-bean-and-marshmallow-square treats!"

Horace groaned.

"You didn't think you'd like the cupcakes," Melody reminded him.

"I suppose you're right," he agreed. He reached under the garbage bag and opened the door of their home.

Melody placed a hand on his arm. "Horace?"

He paused, standing on the doorstep. "Yeah, is something the matter?"

Melody tilted her head. "I promise to try to be less bossy and annoying, okay?"

Horace smiled and nodded. "I'd like that." He pushed the door open and let Melody walk by him into the house.

Melody turned to him as he stepped in and shut the door. "I said I'd *try*. I didn't say I'd succeed." She grinned. "Now go upstairs, change into your regular clothes, then come right back down and set the table for dinner."

Chapter 17

EMPTY HEADS AND HEADLINES

The Splattly family sat around the dining table eating the meal Melody had so carefully prepared. Dr. Splattly sat at one end of the table, Mrs. Splattly sat across from him, and Horace and Melody faced each other.

"Delicious casserole," Dr. Splattly told his daughter.

"Fabulous fries," Mrs. Splattly complimented.

Melody beamed with pride.

"Who would like to begin sharing time?" Dr. Splattly asked. Every night at dinner, the Splattlys had sharing time. All family members had to share a bit of their day and talk about what they were feeling. "Remember," Dr. Splattly told his family, "you don't want to keep too much stuff in your head. Sometimes an empty head is a good head."

Mrs. Splattly addressed the family. "You'll never believe what happened this afternoon. A superhero has appeared in town."

"A superhero?" Melody asked, shooting Horace a mean look.

"What kind of a superhero?" Dr. Splattly asked.

"A purple one," Mrs. Splattly answered. "He came right by my office window. Dozens of people saw him all over town. He saved one girl from a runaway bicycle, and Principal Nosair told me the superhero pulled him out of the stomach of a giant man-eating guinea pig." Mrs. Splattly looked to Horace. "This all sounds like the silly kind of stories you like to make up."

Horace looked down at his plate of food. "Yeah, sure does," he said, holding back a smile.

"If I hadn't seen him myself, I wouldn't have believed it," Mrs. Splattly said. "We're running a front-page story tomorrow. We even have a photo that someone took. No one knows who he is or where he came from."

"Thank goodness," Melody muttered.

Horace heard his sister, but he didn't care. All he could think about was that tomorrow morning, the Cupcaked Crusader would be on the front page of the *Blootinville Banner*. He was a real, live superhero with a secret identity just like all the big-time superheroes. And, even better, everyone would know he was right about the monster in the playground. Tomorrow at school no one would think he, Xax, and Auggie were dorky anymore.

"Horace, did anything interesting happen to you today?" Dr. Splattly asked.

Horace glanced at Melody. She was holding her butter knife low to the table, pointing it at him. "Horace and I just played together nicely all afternoon, right, Horace?" she said sweetly, though her eyes were shooting daggers.

Horace stared his sister down and plastered a smile on his face. "Yup," he answered. "Melody and I are so close we don't keep any secrets from each other. Not even one."

• • •

Later that evening, Horace spied Melody sitting at the kitchen table, working on her diorama of town founder Serena Blootin climbing Rumbly Mountain. It was made out of elbow macaroni, strung with Christmas lights, and flowed with a river of bubbling celernip soda.

While she kept busy, Horace snuck into her room. There on the floor was her Lily Deaver tote bag, open and waiting. He stuck in his hand

and pulled out the package his sister had so carefully wrapped that afternoon—two complete cupcakes and also the two halves Horace hadn't eaten. When Melody noticed them missing, he'd just pretend he didn't know anything about it.

After all, a man as mean as Dienow was sure to do something evil again, wasn't he? And shouldn't a certain superhero have his own cupcakes to defeat him?

Horace walked off to his room and tucked the cupcakes inside a loose wall panel behind his bed. Only he would know where they were hidden. Only he was prepared to fight whatever evil might come to Blootinville.

And Horace knew he could do it.

The Cupcaked Crusader had arrived.

Lawrence David is the author of several picture books and two books for adults. He has never eaten any cupcakes that gave him superpowers, but he hopes to one day. He lives in New York City, where he is always on the lookout for villains, monsters, school bullies, and licorice.

Barry Gott has a twin and was the almost shortest kid in the fourth grade. He longed for superpower-giving cupcakes but never found any. He is the illustrator of a picture book, *Patches Lost and Found*, by Stephen Kroll, and many, many greeting cards. He lives in Ohio.